# A LESSON TO BE
# LEARNED

## E'Loise T. Wallace

Illustrations by Imani A. Bivins

Outskirts Press, Inc.
http://www.outskirtspress.com

Paperback ISBN: 978-1-4787-6440-3
Hardback ISBN: 978-1-4787-7658-1

Interior Illustrations by: Imani A. Bivins.

PRINTED IN THE UNITED STATES OF AMERICA

This Book Belongs to:

The Chesarek family

## Mama, I Know You Are in Heaven

Mom I know that you are in heaven with my Lord
Saying goodbye is so very hard
With pride, I speak your name

Things here will never be the same
There is no one to blame
I know an angel took you by your hand

Although we are apart
You will always be in my heart
Mom I will always love and miss you

This book is dedicated to my loving mom
Juanita Johnson

## Acknowledgements

I believe that our success in life is largely determined by the company we keep. I want to thank everyone who has helped me along the way, especially my niece Miranda Clay, who helped to bring this book to life; my sisters Maxine Clay and Catherine Zeno, who supported me in this effort; and all of my friends, who contributed small things in great ways. Thank you all for reminding me that it is really a big deal to write a book. Thank you for your love and support.

The students are unhappy
as they enter the classroom.

# CHAPTER 1
# Entering the Classroom

In walked Mrs. Wally's students, who constantly complained. "Good morning, Mrs. Wally. Today is supposed to be 'A jingle-jingle an' a honk honk,' a dream come true." "A jingle-jingle an' a honk-honk" is something the students always said when things were going their way.

"Mrs. Wally, did you hear the weather forecast? It was supposed to snow last night, according to the weatherman. Now he says that it is going to snow tonight instead. The weather people make me mad. They don't know anything," said David. The disappointment showed all over the students' faces.

Another student raised his hand to ask a question.

"May I help you, Dennis?" asked Mrs. Wally.

"Yes. Since we are at school today, I think we should have a fun day. I don't want to do any work, just fun stuff."

"What kind of fun stuff are you referring to?" asked Mrs. Wally.

"Hmm, we can play games and watch movies."

"No, that's not a good idea," said David. "I think we should draw our favorite pictures on the board and color them. I won't have to do any homework tonight. Since snow is in the forecast for tomorrow, there will be no school!"

"I just wanted to stay home, but my mom wouldn't let me! Let's do word searches all day long," replied Nikki.

"I want to play the *Jeopardy* games on the computer," said Eartha.

"I will just sit here and let time pass by because I want to go home to play with my new Wii games, and I have a stuffy nose," said Cynthia. "I'll feel better after I bake brownies with my grandma."

"OK, class, let's get ready to begin our school day," replied Mrs. Wally. "We can stay in school and enjoy our day because having fun is a part of our class. Learning can be fun!"

"Yeah, right! That means we have to read and write and work very hard all day long," replied Dennis.

"Yes," said Mrs. Wally, "but it doesn't mean that learning cannot be fun. I am sorry that you students are disappointed about the prediction of snow. I am not convinced that we will have a good day if you all are not motivated or interested. So let me see by a show of hands who will not be actively participating in class today."

All of the students raised their hands, which indicated that this was not going to be a good day.

"I think I have an idea," said Mrs. Wally. "I will be back!" Mrs.Wally rushed to the office, leaving her assistant behind to supervise the class.

# CHAPTER 2

# Mrs. Wally Goes to the Principal's Office

Mrs. Wally went to the principal's office to report that her students were not cooperating. It was obvious that they were not in the mood for learning, so she asked for permission to let her students have an early dismissal. She explained that all of her students were distraught due to the weather advisory.

To Mrs. Wally's surprise, the principal agreed to let her students go home early. Mrs. Doomsday was the principal at Waterway Middle School. She agreed that the students could go home if she received a confirmation from the school's superintendent and verbal permission from parents and guardians. The parents were informed that their children would be returning home within an hour, due to their disruptive behaviors in class. After receiving verbal permission, the secretary called transportation to have a bus return to the school.

Mrs. Wally hurried back to her class to share the good news with the students that they'd been given permission to leave early. She promised each of the students that she would call, once they got home,

Mrs. Wally talks to Principal Doomsday
about an early dismissal.

to see if they were having their anticipated fun. Before the class was dismissed, Mrs. Doomsday explained to the students why they had been given the opportunity to go home early. She expressed her disappointment in the class's choice of poor behavior. She was sorry that they did not display responsible and cooperative student behavior.

"To leave early is a rare exception to the rule," she stated. "You all will be sharing your experience with the Teachers' Support for Learning Committee. The learning committee will use today's early dismissal to study and improve critical thinking in the classroom. Your assignment for this evening is to write a reflection of today's events to be handed in next Monday."

As usual, when things were going their way, the entire class yelled, "That's a jingle-jingle an' a honk-honk!"

They all had smiles on their faces as they prepared to go to their lockers. As they left, Mrs. Wally said good-bye to all the happy faces. When the bus arrived, the students quickly got on board.

Dennis reminded Mrs. Wally, "It's predicted to snow tonight, and there's supposed to be an accumulation of snow."

Mrs. Wally replied, "I just want to remind you before leaving that sometimes you may be faced with additional hurdles to cross or hills to climb before you get what you want. You should be careful about your decisions and your actions."

"There you go with your metaphors again, Mrs. Wally. I know all about similes and metaphors. Remember, I made an A on most of my assignments," said David.

"I'm just saying things could always change and not turn out exactly the way you want them to be. No matter what, there will be a lesson learned. Yes, in most cases you will definitely learn a lesson. Your outcome can be positive or negative, good or bad, happy or sad," warned Mrs. Wally.

The students are very excited when they hear the good news. They all shout, "It's a jingle-jingle an' a honk-honk day!"

Mrs. Wally plans fun lesson activities.

# CHAPTER 3
# Lesson Plans

After the students left, Mrs. Wally began to plan lessons for the next school day. She could only imagine that all of her students were going to be very happy. Hopefully, when they returned, they would listen to their teacher and be cooperative in class. The teacher planned several fun learning activities for her students. She used vocabulary words learned throughout the year to create *Jeopardy* games, word searches, Pictionary, and hangman games. She would also allow the students to create rap songs. Marcus would surely enjoy that! She wanted her students to enjoy learning. For a fun math activity, the students would learn about measurements and division by baking brownies.

Mrs. Wally loved planning fun activities for her students. "Oh yes, I almost forgot; they can play educational games on the iPad and the computer," she said.

"This lesson plan should make my students happy. I cannot wait until they return," thought Mrs. Wally. "They will see that learning can be fun!"

The students are very excited
to go home early.

# CHAPTER 4
# The Bus Ride Home

The school bus was full of joyful noises. There were screams of, "Yes, we are going home to enjoy the snow day off that should've been!" They all shouted, "That's a jingle-jingle an' a honk-honk!" Immediately, the snow began to come down heavily. Mrs. Walker, the bus driver, was having difficulties seeing the lines on the road.

"Why are you driving so slowly?" asked David. "Where did you get your license, from a bubble gum machine?" All of the students began to laugh.

As time passed, David noticed that Mrs. Walker kept hitting the brakes and going very slowly. As he looked out the window, David said, "It's snowing cats and dogs." That was one of the idioms he learned in Mrs. Wally's class. Mrs. Walker apologized for having to drive so slowly. She reminded them that safety is first.

"What time is it?" asked Dennis.

"It is eleven o'clock," said Mrs. Walker. The snow came down harder, and she could not see the road. She was driving at a snail's pace.

All of the students' smiles anxiously turned into worried, concerned faces. No one was talking. They spent most of their time sitting very quietly as they stared out of the window. The blanket of snow covered everything. It became very difficult for them to recognize their route home.

"Don't worry; you all will still have a lot of time to have fun at home," said Mrs. Walker.

Cynthia was falling asleep due to her stuffy nose getting the best of her.

"It looks like a blizzard," said Eartha.

The bus came to a complete stop. Mrs. Walker was trying to use her cell phone to report that she would be stopping on the side of the road until the snow slowed down. She feared that they would be stuck on the side of the road for a long while. Unfortunately, she was not able to reach the transportation office due to poor cell phone reception. She sat calmly along the roadside with her flashers on, trying not to show her distress. Mrs. Walker told the kids she couldn't continue to drive until the snow slowed down.

Eartha became upset and said in a bossy tone, "It better not take a very long time; I'm hungry! I didn't eat any breakfast." However, time passed, it was noon, and they were still on the side of the road.

Marcus remembered that his cell phone was in his book bag. "I have an idea! I will call my parents, and they will come here to get us. They have a big van, and we all can fit in it." He looked at his cell phone; it had only one cell left. "Oh no," said Marcus. "I need to charge my phone." He asked Mrs. Walker if there was a phone plug on the bus.

"Yes, there is a plug near the back of the bus. The question is whether it works," replied Mrs. Walker.

"That's silly, of course the plug works. I will plug in my phone and wait for thirty minutes, and then I will call my mom," said Marcus.

After thirty minutes, he tried to call his mom. He was not able to reach her. Certain that he had waited long enough for his phone to be charged, he continued to call. All of a sudden, he heard a beeping sound coming from his phone. "I must have dialed the wrong number," said Marcus.

Mrs. Walker decided to try using the bus phone again but could not get through. They concluded that the connection was still bad because of the weather. Four hours later, at four o'clock, they thought surely their parents would come for them.

Marcus is surprised when he hears
Mrs. Wally's voice on the cell phone.

# CHAPTER 5
# A Call from Mrs. Wally

Again Marcus heard beeping sounds coming from his phone. Reluctantly he answered, "Hello, who is this?"

"Hello, this is Mrs. Wally."

"How did you get through? There's no service connection. Neither Mrs. Walker nor I could place a call," said Marcus.

"Wow! I am so surprised that I was able to call. I called transportation, but all of the lines were busy," replied Mrs. Wally.

"Well, I guess your call was meant to be," said Marcus. He placed his phone on speaker so everyone could hear Mrs. Wally.

She remembered Marcus had brought his cell phone to class that morning, and it should have been in his locker. She took a chance on calling his phone. "I thought I would try your phone because most of the parents called the school but had no way to communicate with the bus driver. Your phone was my only hope of reaching you all. Your parents are very worried. The road is closed. There is no possible way of getting through until the snow stops."

Mrs. Wally suggested that the students make the best use of a bad situation and try to have as much fun as they could. "Don't worry yourselves; you'll get home soon. Remember, safety is first. You need to keep in mind what I said before you left," said Mrs. Wally.

"What now, Mrs. Wally? Please don't torture us about hurdles to cross or things not turning out the way we want. I don't want to hear that; I am hungry and tired. We remembered what you said just before we got on the bus," said Eartha.

"Yes, I gave you all a thought to ponder. You may be confronted with hurdles to cross before you get what you want. Remember, your outcome can be positive or negative, good or bad, happy or sad. However, there will be a lesson learned," Mrs. Wally kindly reminded them.

With heartfelt sadness, she said, "I am sorry that you all are sitting on the side of the road." Then Mrs. Wally came up with an idea. "Just think about something that you all can do on the bus that is different from being at school having fun."

"Good idea!" said Cynthia. "Although my nose is still very stuffy, I will dream of my grandmother's brownies while I am trying to have fun."

"We promise that we will all try to have a little fun while we sit here!" shouted the students.

# CHAPTER 6

# It was Nine O'Clock, Ten Hours Later

The moonlight glistened on the blanket of snow indicating that it was getting late. The students grew restless and tired.

David suggested, "Let us think of some games we can play while waiting on this awful bus. We need to move around. Let's play a game that will keep us warm. I will get the ball out of my book bag. The rule of the game is to keep the ball moving. You can only keep the ball for a hot second, and if you miss it, you're out."

Nikki chimed, "Ah! I know another game. We can make musical beats by tapping our pencils on our books, and guess the songs."

Hours passed. The students were tired of playing games. "Not many of those games were fun," said Eartha. "Oh no, maybe weee...should have been in school. Just like Mrs. Wally said, 'Learning can be fun.'"

"Since we are stuck here, I need to try to drive this bus. I would hit the gas, turn the wheel, and get us out of here. We would be home in no time!" said David.

Mrs. Walker keeps her cool after waiting ten hours on the bus with a bunch of unhappy children.

"Yeah, right," said Eartha. "We would be in the ditch, turned over! We should think good, positive thoughts, the way Mrs. Wally reminded us to do in the classroom."

"We are still on a bus without heat," said Cynthia. "I am cold. Could you please turn up the heat, Mrs. Walker? Or keep the engine running so we can stay warm?"

Mrs. Walker replied, "We are low on fuel."

"Great," said Nikki. "That's all we need is to be here all night on the bus in the cold without gas. We need to concentrate on getting our homework done so we can turn it in to Mrs. Doomsday. We can't really write about the fun we had, but this is definitely a lesson learned."

"Let's write about the lesson we learned by not staying at school," replied Marcus. "We can write about the fun we missed by wanting to go back home."

"If we finish our assignment on time, what are we getting?" asked Cynthia. "I mean, did Mrs. Doomsday say that we can get a prize or extra credit for helping her dumb committee?"

Dennis sat there quietly listening to the others complain. In a serious tone, he yelled, "Now we get to contribute to a committee that studies the real-life situations of students since we were not willing to cooperate in class. We got to go home early and now look—I'm stuck in the snow for ten hours with a bunch of whiny babies!"

"We got what we deserved, whether it turned out to be a good or not-so-good experience," said Eartha. "If we had stayed at school, at least Mrs. Wally has food and water in her classroom."

All of the students began to cry.

All of a sudden, after spending hours on the bus, the snow stopped. Mrs. Walker was able to contact transportation. The bus was buried in two feet of snow. She needed a snowplow to pull the bus out of the deep snow. The cries turned into sounds of laughter, and the students yelled, "That's a jingle-jingle an' a honk-honk!" They were so glad to be going home even though they only had time to sleep and return to school. When they got home, many were happy that they got their assignments completed on the bus, especially Eartha. The snow prediction for the next day was canceled, and ironically they all were excited to return to school.

"Yay!" the students showed mixed emotions as they were rescued.

# CHAPTER 7
# Students Return to Share Their Experiences

The school bell rang and in walked the students. Mrs. Wally greeted her students with a soft "Good morning. It is a dream come true to be back at school. It is going to be a jingle-jingle an' a honk-honk day." Surprisingly, the students came to school that day without complaining.

"We had a rough time on that bus yesterday," one student cried.

"It was a nightmare in the daytime," said Marcus.

"An experience that I would not wish on my worst enemy," said Cynthia.

"We took your advice, Mrs. Wally," they shouted. "We played games to keep us warm."

"Mrs. Wally, you would have been very proud of me. I took my ball from my book bag," said David.

"Eartha helped us keep calm. She reminded us of what you said just before we got on the bus. She got us on track so we could finish our homework assignment," said Nikki.

"We have written about our bus ride and not having any fun at all. We finally understand your reminder…that sometimes the outcome of our decisions can make us happy or sad. It could be negative or positive," said Dennis.

"I'm glad not to be stuck on the side of the road. The bus was running out of gas," said Nikki, "and silly David wanted to drive the bus faster than Mrs. Walker."

"I did not miss playing games at home," said Dennis. "I was so tired when I got home that I went to sleep right away."

On the bus, the students had decided to apologize to Mrs. Wally for being upset and not cooperating in class.

"The weatherman wasn't correct in predicting the weather. We know that people make mistakes! We have to roll with the punches," said David. There he went again with another one of his idioms! "As we sat on that bus for hours, we began to see the heavy snow coming down harder and harder. We realized that our dreams of having fun at home had gone down the drain," David said. "Another idiom! I guess you can tell that I like learning about idioms."

The students learned a valuable lesson about being in the wrong place at the wrong time. The truth was they were stuck on a cold bus, without food, all because they wanted to leave school early with hopes of having fun at home. The students gave a great big "jingle-jingle an' a honk-honk" shout-out.

All of the students are eager to share their stories as they read their reflections of being stuck on the bus.

# CHAPTER 8

# Lesson Learned: Reflections

"It's time to share your positive and negative reflections, along with your quotes of your learned experiences," said Mrs. Wally. "Mrs. Doomsday will share them with the Teachers' Support for Learning Committee."

## Nikki

Positive: I learned that sticking together during tough times is a good thing. I was pleased to help Cynthia because she had a stuffy nose.

Negative: We should have stayed at school and looked at the weather report before leaving.

Quote: *Being in a hurry to do anything can make you miss a step.*

## David

Positive: I learned, just as I had fun learning about idioms and metaphors in class, that I would have had more fun staying in school than being stuck on the bus playing games.

Negative: Speaking rudely to Mrs. Walker and criticizing the way she drove the bus was a mistake.

I should have been patient. Also, pulling together to keep pieces in place is better than having one odd piece that doesn't fit anywhere.

Quote: *Laughter and jokes are OK. You need to choose the right time.*

### Cynthia

Positive: I have learned that being stuck on a cold bus in the snow is worse than having a stuffy nose.

Negative: I used my stuffy nose as an excuse not to do my assignment in class.

Quote: *Sickness can be caused by many things, especially being trapped with limited choices.*

### Eartha

Positive: I learned how to be optimistic and to always do what I can do. I try to make good choices during tough situations. I am learning all of the time, even when I'm having fun or it doesn't seem like I am learning.

Negative: Not thinking positively when you can.

Quote: *Going too fast when you are crossing hurdles can make you forget to leap high.*

### Marcus

Positive: I have learned that my cell phone should have been in the locker and I didn't follow directions, but Mrs. Wally could not have contacted us without it.

Negative: I need to charge my phone the night before class.

Quote: *Depending on others to rescue you during difficult times will get you nowhere.*

## Dennis

Positive: I have learned not to suggest having fun at school instead of being prepared to learn.

Negative: Causing a disturbance in class is not a good idea.

Quote: *Your words can cause others to agree and even react.*


"You all have written such great reflections and quotes. I am sure of that. Mrs. Doomsday will be happy to share them with her committee. Oh, I almost forgot; she said your reflections and quotes will be entered into a contest. You can win extra educational games for the iPad, and computer," said Mrs. Wally.

They all shouted, "That's a jingle-jingle an' a honk-honk." That is what Mrs. Wally's students always said when things were going their way.

Mrs. Wally included this quote.

"Keep your thoughts positive because your
   thoughts become your words.
Keep your words positive because your words
   become your behaviors.
Keep your behaviors positive because your
   behaviors become your habits.
Keep your habits positive because your habits
   become your values.
Keep your values positive because your values
   become your destiny."

~Mahatma Gandhi

# The End

CPSIA information can be obtained
at www.ICGtesting.com
Printed in the USA
BVHW021346280219
541427BV00017B/512/P

*9 7 8 1 4 7 8 7 7 6 5 8 1 *